540L

D1237280

MICHAEL DAHL'S

REALLY SCARY STORIES

Michael Dahl's Really Scary Stories
are published by Stone Arch Books
A Capstone Imprint
1710 Roe Crest Drive
North Mankato, Minnesota 56003
www.mycapstone.com

Library of Congress Cataloging-in-Publication Data

Names: Dahl, Michael, author. | Bonet, Xavier, 1979- illustrator. | Dahl,
   Michael. Really scary stories.
Title: The library claw : and other scary tales / by Michael Dahl ;
   illustrated by Xavier Bonet.
Description: North Mankato, Minnesota : Stone Arch Books, a Capstone imprint,
   [2017] | Series: Michael Dahl's really scary stories | Summary: In
   Ravenville's library there is a special, hidden room for biographies of
   local people, but when Darren enters the room looking for a book to use
   for a homework assignment he discovers that there is something hungry
   living among the shelves, and people who enter rarely come out—and that
   is only one of the scary stories in this collection.
Identifiers: LCCN 2017002242 (print) | LCCN 2017003310 (ebook) | ISBN
   9781496549020 (library binding) | ISBN 9781496549068 (ebook pdf)
Subjects: LCSH: Libraries—Juvenile fiction. | Monsters—Juvenile fiction. |
   Horror tales. | Children's stories, American. | CYAC: Horror stories. |
   Short stories. | LCGFT: Horror fiction.
Classification: LCC PZ7.D15134 Li 2017 (print) | LCC PZ7.D15134 (ebook) | DDC
   813.54 [Fic] — dc23
LC record available at https://lccn.loc.gov/2017002242

Designer: Tracy McCabe
Image Credits: Shutterstock: Dmitry Natashin, black box design element

Printed and bound in China.
010336F17

THE
LIBRARY
CLAW
AND OTHER SCARY TALES

By Michael Dahl

Illustrated by
Xavier Bonet

STONE ARCH BOOKS
a capstone imprint

TABLE OF CONTENTS

Natalie's family had been living there for two weeks when she heard the noise. She had just gone to bed when she heard a creak.

The moaning had stopped, and the boy no longer heard the flip-flip-flop of the dog's happy tail.

She shivered. Although Jonica loved being onstage and getting all the attention and applause during a show, an empty theater was creepy.

Dear Reader,

Growing up I often visited my aunt's house, where my cousin Cheryl and I would play upstairs in Cheryl's room.

Halfway up the stairs sat my aunt's ornate bookshelf with glass doors. It was filled with old books and their colorful covers. There was one dark blue cover I'll never forget.

On its spine was an image of a genie. Not a friendly genie, though. This creature was half man, half monster, with large outstretched hands. It looked like a book that would take hold of you and not let go.

I was too afraid to walk past that bookshelf.

Cheryl would turn the book around so the edge with the pages faced out, and then I could walk up the staircase.

JUST REMEMBER, YOU NEVER KNOW WHAT YOU MIGHT FIND ON THE LIBRARY SHELF . . .

Michael Dahl

THE BOY IN THE BASEMENT

Ten-year old Natalie stood at the top of the basement stairs. A single bulb hung above the last step. The rest of the basement remained in thick shadow.

Natalie gripped the banister. She took a few cautious steps down. Was that a moving shadow beyond the circle of light? Were her tired eyes playing tricks?

No, she told herself. *There's nothing there. Nothing. There.*

She backed up the steps and firmly closed the door.

When her family had first moved into the old

house a few weeks ago, Natalie had found a piece of blue paper in her closet. The room had belonged to the girl who had lived here before. Natalie figured the paper must have belonged to the girl, something she had forgotten. She unfolded the paper and saw six words written in faint handwriting: *Feed the boy in the basement.*

Natalie's body had gone cold.

During that first week in the new house, she accompanied her father and her brothers, Mike and Kalen, when they carried boxes to store down there. The basement had a cold stone floor. The brick walls were painted white. Old-fashioned lights hung from the ceiling, the kind that you switched on by pulling a small chain. Natalie was tall for her age, but she was still too short to reach the chains. She decided that first week she would never go downstairs alone.

Instead, each night at dinner, she would think of the message on the paper. *Feed the boy in the basement.*

After dinner, Natalie would open the door to the basement and stare down into the darkness. She didn't know why she did it. Maybe to prove to herself that the message had been a joke. It might have been part of a story the unknown girl had written.

No one could live in the basement, she told herself. Her parents or her brothers would have seen something.

* * *

Natalie's family had been living there for two weeks when she heard the noise. She had just gone to bed when she heard a creak. The basement door was opening.

Natalie shivered and snuggled into her bed. She heard the sound of footsteps walking across the kitchen floor. The footsteps stopped outside her door. *This can't be happening,* thought Natalie.

Something scratched on the door. Natalie felt like screaming, but she was too scared. She gripped the covers, her hands clammy with sweat, as her bedroom door slowly opened. A shadow stood there.

"Feed me. . . . ," it said.

Natalie screamed and shot under the covers.

Then she heard laughter. The light switched on.

She looked up and saw her two brothers shaking with laughter.

"I knew that would get you," said Mike.

Natalie's face was red. "You two are super mean!" she said angrily.

"Mike found the note in your closet when we were moving boxes into your room," said Kalen, grinning. "He left it there, but then we thought it was the perfect prank."

"We weren't sure if you had read it or not," said Mike.

"Then we saw you looking down the basement stairs after dinner every night," said Kalen. "And we knew."

"It was perfect," said Mike. "Perfect."

Natalie jumped out of bed. "How do you know there *isn't* a boy in the basement?"

Mike rolled his eyes. "We've been down there a hundred times."

"So?" said Natalie.

"C'mon," said Kalen. "I'll show you."

The three siblings walked into the kitchen. Mike flipped the light switch. Kalen reached into the cookie jar on the counter and grabbed two chocolate chip cookies.

"Are you watching?" said Kalen. He opened the basement door and hopped down the steps.

Mike was still laughing. "Don't waste those cookies," he called down.

Kalen looked up at the two of them. "Watch," he said. He held the cookies like he would a Frisbee and tossed them both into a dark corner.

"Hope he likes them," said Mike.

Natalie leaned forward. She hadn't heard the sound of the cookies falling on the floor.

"He'd better," said Kalen. "It's Mom's recipe."

Kalen turned at a sound. From the top of the stairs, Natalie and Mike saw a long, slithery pink tongue shoot out of the shadows. It wrapped itself three or four times around Kalen, then pulled him into the dark.

There was a nasty smacking sound, followed by a low purr. Without meaning to, they had fed the boy in the basement.

SKIPPY

Dinner was not going well. Milo kept stealing glances at his mother and father, back and forth across the table, across the soup. His mother and father were not speaking. They hardly made any noise at all. They were too busy listening.

They were listening to sounds coming from the kitchen. Milo, however, ignored the moaning and the huffing. He ignored the churning sound of food spilling all over the tile floor. He ignored the *flip-flip-flop* of the dog's tail happily hitting the wall. It was a noisy reminder that Skippy had knocked over and broken seventeen separate items in the last week.

Milo's father set his spoon down, resting it

against the rim of his soup bowl. He took a deep breath. "Skippy —" he began.

"Skippy is good!" Milo said. He was surprised that he spoke so suddenly, so loudly. His father was surprised too. He gave Milo the look he sometimes gave to his laptop when he was having computer problems.

He began again. "Skippy is —"

His mother interrupted. "Yes, dear, Skippy *is* a good dog. But he has problems."

A very gross sound came from the kitchen.

"Lots of problems," said his father.

Milo knew that his parents were right. One of Skippy's problems was hard to ignore. He would forget to bark at the back door so he could do his business outside. Little brown surprises appeared on rugs and carpets throughout the house.

"Did you know," Milo had said one afternoon after school, "that over in Paris they call dog poop *la chocolate*? We learned that in French class. So that means Milo is trying to be nice and give us treats."

"Well, *la chocolate* belongs outside!" his father had said. "Not in the house."

No sense of humor, Milo had thought.

Sitting at the dinner table, Milo was hoping that Skippy had not deposited another treat in the kitchen.

It was his mom's turn to sigh. She looked at Milo's dad and said, "I think we should tell him."

"Tell him?" asked Milo. "Tell him what? I mean, tell *me* what?"

His dad pushed his chair away from the table. "As you know," he said, "Skippy is becoming more . . . challenging. He's making messes and biting. He's breaking things and running up and down the stairs —"

"But he doesn't always do bad things," said Milo.

"Maybe not," said his father. "But he's getting worse."

His mother frowned. "Skippy is just not working out."

"What do you mean?" said Milo. But he knew what they meant. It was happening again.

His mother looked at the kitchen clock. "Let's get it over with," she said.

Milo's father stood up and walked into the kitchen. His mother followed. Milo sat still. The same thing was happening that had happened to several of his former pets. He did not want to watch. He stared at his soup, but he didn't see it. He was trying so hard to think of another solution and was wishing he were far away.

His mother stepped quickly back into the room. She stood behind Milo and said, "Don't come outside, dear. You might get struck or have something hit your head. You know how these things are. It's . . . it's easier this way." Then she was gone.

Milo heard the back door open and his parents walk outside. The moaning had stopped, and the boy no longer heard the *flip-flip-flop* of the dog's happy tail. He knew Skippy was with them.

Milo kept sitting. His parents would be walking through the backyard, getting farther away from the house now. They needed room.

Suddenly, Milo needed room. He couldn't breathe as he sat there, waiting. He jumped up from the table. He ran outside and saw his parents standing in the grass, his father holding on to the little, struggling dog.

"Milo!" shouted his mother.

"Go back in the house," his father ordered.

It was too late. It was happening. Milo heard the sound and looked up. There it was. Like a fat black spider, a delivery drone from the pet hub hovered. It buzzed like a wasp as it eased down to the ground. Its six thin arms held a box.

Milo stood back. Drones didn't always slow down in time to make their landing. Sometimes their arms twitched and boxes fell out of the sky. He had a friend whose family had ordered a new refrigerator. It had landed on their car.

This drone flew smoothly. Skippy would soon be sailing back to the pet hub. The hub's popular return policy said if there was any error with one of their robot forever friends, they would take it back. No questions asked. Full refund. Milo knew that his father would place Skippy inside the box, snap the lid shut, and watch the drone carry Skippy back to the factory.

Milo's family had bad luck with pets. The cuddly

black kitten named Pouncer spit electrical sparks when it purred. The lop-eared rabbit drilled through walls. The cinnamon-colored pug had a weight issue. It floated at random moments throughout the house, bumping against the ceiling, breaking lamps, drifting through cobwebs. Milo had thought it was cool having a flying pet, but his parents were having none of it.

His father thought their house was too close to the power lines. His mother, who watched a lot of horror films, suggested that ghosts were playing tricks on them.

Milo didn't know what the problem was, he just knew he was never going to have a pet like his friends did. He walked slowly back toward the house and heard the bark behind him. That wasn't Skippy's bark. Skippy was already on his way back to the store.

"Milo," said his mother.

The boy turned and ran to his parents. His father was holding a dog, a different dog. The dog was small and brown and squirmy. "It's alive!" exclaimed Milo. He held out his arms and took the puppy from his father. "It's a real live dog," he said.

His mother smiled. "We knew how much you wanted a pet," she said. "And the robots were just not working out."

"But live ones are so expensive," said Milo.

His father was smiling too. "Not a problem, son," he said.

Milo nuzzled the puppy as he carried it toward the house.

His mother looked fondly at the boy. She noticed that his left leg kept swinging out at an odd angle. His head rotated once on his shoulders, then adjusted itself. His left ear made a popping sound and fell off as the boy closed the door behind him. *More Milo problems,* thought his mother.

She looked at her husband and said, "I think we should tell him."

He nodded. "I'll call the factory in the morning."

THE
WIZARD
OF
AHHHHHHS!

Jonica screamed in terror.

But it was a bad scream, and it wasn't at the right time.

"No, no," said Mrs. Cartright, jumping up from her seat in the audience. "You scream *after* the flying monkeys land, not before. Wait till their paws hit the ground."

Jonica had always dreamed of playing Dorothy in *The Wizard of Oz*. But now that she had the role in her school play, she wasn't so sure she really wanted it. Dorothy was in every scene. She had a lot of lines to remember. And she had to remember when to stand, when to sit, when to speak. When you pick up Toto, hold him at your side, not in front of you. Always have your face half turned toward the audience so they can hear you. It was a lot harder than she had imagined. As if that weren't enough, the ruby slippers were too tight.

They did the scene again, and Jonica got the timing of the scream right. It still wasn't a good scream. She was feeling tired. The whole cast was tired. And to top it off, the rope that held one of the flying monkeys had broken, and the monkey had landed on top of the Cowardly Lion.

"All right, everyone," said Mrs. Cartright. "I think that's good for tonight. Terrific work. Alex, your makeup needs a little work. You look like a zombie, not the Tin Man. We'll have to work on that. OK, cast. Tomorrow right after school, we get to work again."

Jonica joined the other girls in their dressing room. She thought about changing out of her costume and wig, taking off the uncomfortable slippers, and putting on her regular clothes. But she was so tired.

Jonica plopped down in the big armchair against the wall. She thought, *I'm just going to close my eyes for a little while.*

She said goodbye to the other girls as they left, but she didn't open her eyes.

When she did open them a while later, she jumped up. She looked at the clock over the door. She had slept for more than an hour! Her parents would be worried.

Crash!

It sounded like something had fallen onto the stage. Jonica rushed out of the dressing room, still wearing her costume. Had the set fallen over? Did part of the roof cave in? Jonica wound her way through the props and the scenery — all of which looked normal — and reached the front of the stage. Nothing was out of place. Nothing had fallen. The stage was empty and quiet, like the rest of the auditorium. In fact, Jonica was the only person there.

She shivered. Although Jonica loved being onstage and getting all the attention and applause during a show, an empty theater was creepy.

She headed back to the dressing room. Her house was a few streets away. It wouldn't take her long to reach home once she had changed out of her costume. Jonica wound her way back through the scenery. She passed cardboard trees and Styrofoam crows. The flying monkeys were hanging from wires overhead. The castle of the Wicked Witch was merely a painting on a big flat of canvas.

Where was the dressing room? It was taking her a lot longer to go back than it had to run onto the stage. Jonica hadn't realized there were so many props. So many trees. The scenery was actually quite good. There were some truly talented kids in set design, she decided. The painted scenes of thick forest and distant mountains looked beautiful. Realistic. They looked so real she imagined the branches waving in the wind and clouds drifting past the mountains. Were those birds twittering among the trees?

She saw the scenery was clearing up ahead. *Finally,* Jonica thought. But a few steps later, she walked out from the shadow of the trees and into a forest clearing. Grass cushioned her feet. Stars twinkled in a deep blue sky. The tree branches *were* waving in a gentle warm breeze.

Where am I? she thought.

She was not outside the school. She hadn't walked through a doorway. If she were outside the school, she would've seen lights from the houses in her neighborhood. But the only light was starlight, and the glow of a moon somewhere behind the trees.

"Oh!" Jonica stepped on something soft. She bent down and saw a small, dark shape. She put out her hand and felt fluffy ears. It was Toto, the prop dog she used as Dorothy's faithful pet. Stuffing was falling out of the fake fur. *Who would rip it apart like this?* Jonica wondered. She remembered how her real dog, Stella, had chewed up one of her favorite stuffed animals. This was worse.

Something gleamed beyond the trees on the other side of the clearing. Out stepped the Tin Man carrying his ax.

"Alex," she said. "Alex, is that you?"

This Tin Man was much taller than Alex, who played the part. And it wasn't Alex's costume. This tin head looked more like an iron helmet. Starlight shone on sharp edges and spikes sprouting all over its body. This Tin Man's nose was a long drill. Its red eyes glowed like distant traffic lights.

"Where's Alex?" Jonica shouted.

The Tin Man came closer. Jonica saw something red on the edge of the huge ax. What was going on? Where was she?

The Tin Man raised his weapon.

"Don't!" shouted Jonica.

Just as suddenly, the figure dropped the ax. Slowly he backed away from Jonica, step by step, until he was lost in the shadows of the trees.

"What was that all about?" she said aloud.

A deep growl rumbled behind her and rippled through her body. Jonica turned to see a massive lion stalking toward her. A real lion. It flattened itself against the grass. The real grass. The mighty creature balanced on its great paws. Black claws gleamed in the starlight. It was getting ready to pounce.

Jonica remembered the ax lying in the grass directly behind her. If she was careful . . . if she could just reach back and . . .

Jonica screamed in terror.

This time it was a good scream. And her last.

MEMBER OF THE BAND

The orange door opened with a rusty squeal, like an animal in pain.

"Sounds like B sharp," joked Cameron.

"Sounds more like someone dying," said Jesse.

The two boys, carrying their black clarinet cases, entered the old Serling Middle School building. The halls were empty. Dust and old papers littered the floors between rows of lockers on either side, the narrow doors firmly shut.

"Hello!" said Cam.

Hello, hello, hello, returned the echo from the empty hallways and hollow classrooms.

"This place is spooky. Anyway, I think the band room is that way." Cam pointed.

The boys walked toward the end of the long hall. "That echo was creepy," whispered Jesse. "It didn't sound like your voice."

"Sure it did," said Cam. "It's an echo." He burst out with another "Hello!"

Hello, hello, hello . . .

A fire had damaged the boys' regular school, so classes and sports practices were shifted to several other schools in the district. After weeks without rehearsals, the music director, Mr. Garfield, finally found the band a new home. They were using the old rehearsal room in the empty Serling building.

Cam and Jesse could see light slanting out of a doorway up ahead. They heard chairs and music stands scraping against tile floor. Mr. Garfield and some students were probably setting up the room for practice.

"Hey, what's that?" said Jesse. He began walking down a dim hall that led away from the band room. Cam followed.

"Check it out!" said Jesse. "It's an old mural."

The mural took up an entire wall. It showed students with their musical instruments. The entire mural was fading. Above the crowd of musicians floated a banner that read: FOLLOW THE BAND.

"Ha," Jesse said with a snort. "Guess what Mr. Garfield is going to say?" He pointed to the faded figure of a boy carrying a saxophone.

"We need a saxophone," Cam replied. "That's what he always says. Every rehearsal. 'Doesn't anyone want to learn the saxophone?'"

The boys heard more band members arriving, so they walked back to the rehearsal room. As they stepped away from the glass cabinets and the old mural, Cam thought he heard a soft sound behind him. The sad wail of a saxophone far, far away.

But during rehearsal, Cam forgot about the mural. He was caught up in the challenge of making his clarinet blend together with all the other instruments in the band. At different points in the song, different musicians or sections would carry the melody. Mr. Garfield was always fun. He energetically led them through piece after piece, until he put his baton down for the last time. Cam couldn't believe that two hours had passed.

"Great work, clarinets," said Mr. Garfield to the

five clarinet players. "Lovely sound. I just wish . . . Doesn't anyone want to learn the saxophone?"

Cam and Jesse looked at each other and laughed.

As the director shouted out times and dates for the next rehearsals, the students were busy putting away their instruments, snapping cases shut, shuffling sheets of music, or hoisting huge bags over their shoulders.

Cam whispered to Jesse, "I've gotta make a pit stop. Wait here for me."

Jesse nodded.

Cam wandered for several minutes before finding the restrooms. As soon as he had finished and stepped out from the bathroom, he sensed something was different. The hallways seemed darker. All the lockers were open. Their narrow metal doors had swung loose. They were full of shadows. Cam was certain they had been closed before he'd used the restroom.

He sprinted to the band room. The lights had been turned off and everyone was gone. "What's going on?" he said to the empty room. Only his clarinet case, still sitting on his chair, remained. The boy rushed to the doorway and yelled, "Jess!"

Jess, Jess, Jess . . .

Silence, and then —

"Down here. By the mural."

"I told you to wait for me," said Cam, rushing down the hallway. Wait. Where was Jesse? The hall was empty.

He called his friend's name again. No answer this time. He walked farther down the hall. Shadows hovered like a fog. The exit sign at the far end of the hall was smashed and dark. Cam tried opening the door, but it was stuck. He backed up and shouldered it hard. It didn't budge. He'd have to exit the way he came in, through the squeaky orange door.

Cameron did not especially like the dark. He gripped his clarinet case firmly and began to run. *Once past the cabinets,* he told himself, *turn to the right, and you'll see the orange door.* But as he approached the mural, he saw dozens of hands and arms reaching out from the wall. It was too late to stop. He tried to swerve, but the arms were long. A crowd of hands swarmed around his body, pulling at his clothes, his hair, his instrument case. Fingers wiggled and clawed.

Just as suddenly, it all stopped. Cam felt cold. Darkness closed in around him.

He wanted to yell for Jesse again, but when he opened his mouth, nothing came out. A small light caught his attention. It seemed to be a tiny window. No, as he walked closer, he realized it was a pair of eyeholes in the wall. Level with his own. Cam cautiously put his face to the holes and gazed out.

He was staring into the very hall where he had stood a moment before. It was no longer empty. A boy wearing faded blue jeans, a faded green sweater, and faded brown shoes was staring at Cam. In his hand he carried a faded black instrument case. Cam recognized the case. It was for a saxophone.

The kid looked so happy, happier than anyone Cam had ever seen before. The boy smiled. "I've waited so long for my turn," he said. "But don't worry." He turned toward Cam. "I'll be back. You'll all get your chance."

Cam couldn't move. He was frozen in place. The boy with the saxophone walked down the hallway and out of sight. Cam was part of a new band now.

THE PHANTOM TRAIN

Patricia had half a mind to stop pedaling her bike and lie down in the nearby grass. She was worn out.

"Does it ever end?" Patricia shouted to her cousin, who was riding up ahead.

"You're always so impatient," said Ross. "This road will take us right past the cow barn."

The two cousins had been biking for hours, exploring the roads and highways that skirted the boundaries of Ross's farm. Now their shadows grew longer. The sky was a deeper blue. The breeze was cool, and Patricia's legs were tired.

"It's not far now," called Ross.

The soft dirt Patricia had been riding on suddenly turned hard, gray, and flat. Ross was leading her down an old highway. Up ahead she saw two train signals, their long white arms pointing into the air.

Suddenly, the signals came alive. The orange lights flashed. Their bells rang out loud and clear as the white guard arms lowered in front of them.

Ross came to a stop and stood with his head lowered, concentrating. "There's no train coming," he said.

"How do you know?" asked Patricia, pulling up beside him.

"The ground should be rumbling," he said. "We'd feel it if a train was coming."

The bells kept clanging.

"Then why —" she began.

"Who knows?" said Ross. "Some kind of malfunction." He steered his bike to the end of the first guard. "Let's just go around," he said. Patricia followed him, and they both walked their bikes to the side of the road.

"Hey!"

The kids turned and saw a car beside them. The shout came from a middle-aged man, who sat behind the steering wheel. He was sunburned and wrinkled, with a worn cap on his head. Patricia thought his car looked like it belonged in an old movie. It had fins and chrome and was painted white and turquoise.

"You kids don't want to be fooling with that train track," said the man. He didn't look at them. He stared straight ahead, gazing beyond the guard arms. "You haven't heard about the Phantom Train?" he asked.

Ross rolled his eyes.

"I haven't heard of it," said Patricia.

The man stared straight ahead. "Years back," he began, "a young man was speeding along these parts, spinning up dust for miles. Then he came down this road. Halfway Road, it's called."

"I didn't know it had a name," said Ross.

"Don't know why Halfway," said the man. "Maybe because it's halfway between here and the devil."

The man continued telling his story and kept staring straight ahead. *Maybe he's lying,* thought

Patricia. Her grandma had told her that liars never look you straight in the eye.

"The kid reached this here train track," said the man. "And a train was coming. You could feel it rumble in the air. The lights were on. The rails were coming down. But the kid didn't stop. He stepped on the gas and went faster. He figured he was smart enough and his car was fast enough to beat the train. If the rails came down, so be it, he thought. He'd crash right through 'em."

Patricia couldn't wait for him to take a breath. "And did he?" she asked. "Did he crash through them?"

"Indeed he did," said the man. "Crashed through the first rail like a knife through butter and ran smack into the side of the coming train. CRACK! The car got caught somehow, stuck to the side of the train. Dragged the car and that poor kid almost a mile before the train was able to stop."

Patricia thought she was going to be sick.

"When they pulled the car off the train . . ." The man paused to swallow. "When they pulled the car off, they found the kid."

Ross's eyes grew wide. "They did?"

"Yeah, and know what they found? His body was cut right in half. From his skull down to his legs. Like two halves of an apple with the seeds showing. Like something out of a nightmare. And that's where the Phantom Train comes from. Every so often, people who drive down this road will see the arms come down and the lights flash. And if they wait a minute, they'll feel the wind from the train."

Patricia's hair began to blow in the breeze.

"They'll feel the rumble from the tracks."

Patricia and Ross felt a vibration in their handlebars.

"That's when you know the Phantom Train is coming," said the man. "A train you don't want to mess with." He stared straight ahead through the windshield, hypnotized by the signals.

Ross turned to Patricia. "Good story," he mumbled under his breath.

"It ain't a story! I saw it!" shouted the man. "I was there!" He turned to look at them. The man's head was split in half. His face had only one eye, a single flaring nostril, and crooked teeth hanging in half of his mouth. The other side, the side that had been facing away from them, wasn't there.

Patricia screamed. She got on her bike and headed to the train crossing. She had to get away.

Ross pulled her back, just as the breeze became a wind, and the wind swirled into a gale. A wall of air swept over them, pushing them back from the guard arms. Light flooded the tracks. A train's horn blared across the empty fields, louder than thunder. And as the cousins watched, a huge shadow in the shape of a train rocketed past them. It whipped at their clothes and flattened the grass that surrounded them. Patricia screamed a second time as she watched this machine from another world speeding over the tracks.

They closed their eyes against the dust and gravel swirling around them, until the wind slowly loosened its grasp. The lights were gone. The train had vanished. Ross jumped when the guard arms suddenly lifted. Finally the bells stopped.

The two cousins stared at each other.

Ross broke the long silence and turned toward the car. "Thanks, mister," he said. "You saved our lives."

But the car was no longer there. The road was empty.

THE
LIBRARY
CLAW

Darren didn't realize the town library had a second hidden library inside it. Not until he had to go there and rescue someone.

In fact, he rarely went inside the building, though it was hard to miss. It sat in the center of Ravenville, like a spider at the center of its web. The huge, sprawling, three-story pile of brick and stone was more than two hundred years old. Over the years, the townspeople added rooms, wings, turrets, fireplaces, and staircases to it until the library that Darren knew covered an entire city block.

He trudged up the stone stairs to the entrance. He had only two days left to turn in a report for history class. He hadn't even started working on it. He had to write about a person who lived in Ravenville during the 1800s.

Boring, thought Darren.

Inside the library's main entrance, Darren got a surprise. His heart began pounding so hard he was afraid people might hear it.

He had caught a glimpse of his classmate, Dawn Potter. Dawn Potter, the prettiest girl he had ever spoken to. He hadn't said a lot to her. He'd only said, "It's page twenty-six," when Dawn had asked what page number the teacher was talking about once. But he put as much feeling into those three words as he could possibly muster.

She's working on the same assignment, Darren thought. *Maybe I should ask her about her report, or where she got her information.* That would give him an excuse to talk to her. Darren watched Dawn join two girls at a table in one of the reading rooms. *Great! There goes my chance,* he thought. He couldn't talk to her with the other girls around.

Darren wandered around the huge building. He climbed stairs, explored hallways, and looked at the endless stacks of books. He was hunting for the biography section.

At an information desk, he found a librarian, a young man wearing retro glasses and a preppy sweatshirt. When Darren asked about biographies, the librarian asked if he was looking for something more specific.

"Yeah," said Darren. "Someone who lived in town. And they had to live in the 1800s."

A gleam appeared in the man's eyes. "Really? In Ravenville?"

That's what Darren had said.

"Oh, this will be cool," said the librarian, coming around his desk. "Follow me."

Darren had no idea how enormous the library was. He lost count of the hallways and staircases. How far was Mr. Librarian taking him?

When they had gone down several flights of steps, the librarian stopped at a blank wall. It was paneled in smooth honey-colored wood.

Darren said, "It's a wall."

The librarian smiled and shook his head. He put his hands against the wall and pushed. A hidden door swung inward. Darren could see rays of dusty sunlight trying to penetrate the gloom. The man took a few steps forward, gesturing toward the dimness.

Walking farther in, Darren saw a tall room filled floor-to-ceiling with rows and rows of shelves. Hundreds, probably of thousands, of old books filled the shelves. Piles of ancient volumes lay scattered on the floor like miniature pyramids.

"I believe, *this* is the biography section you're looking for," said the librarian. "These are all biographies of people who settled or lived in Ravenville from 1790 to 1880. This is the perfect place for you."

"Where exactly are we?" asked Darren.

"The library, of course." He hesitated. "But this is part of the Inner Library. Very old, very old. Not many people come down here anymore. It's reserved for our . . . *special* patrons." He turned away and walked toward the exit. "I'll leave the door open," he added.

"Uh, thanks," said Darren, but when he turned around, the librarian was already gone.

Darren found that the rows were labeled by year. It shouldn't be too hard to find someone from the right time period. He walked in and out of shadows, working his way farther into the maze. One section intrigued him. It was next to one of the walls, and was closed off by a musty velvet rope. It was easy enough to step over. Darren scanned the books. They were ancient, all right. Probably about the oldest people who had lived in the town. Darren was struck by how thin they all were. *Good, not too much to read,* he thought. He noticed that instead of titles, names were printed along the spines. *Becker . . . Biltmore . . . Brannigan . . .*

One's as good as another, thought Darren.

He reached for a book, and then stopped. Out of the corner of his eye he saw a shadow. A shape passed swiftly at the end of the row. "Is someone else here?" he called out. When there was no answer, Darren walked to the end of the row, leaned over the velvet rope, and glanced in each direction. No one.

He went back to the shelf and grabbed a book. It didn't have a title. Darren held the book in both hands. Something moved. He heard what he thought was breathing. In and out. In and out. With each breath, the book seemed to pulse in his hands. The boy carefully opened it.

He cried out in surprise.

On one of the pages was a picture of Dawn. It wasn't drawn or painted on. It was a photograph. Underneath he saw two dates written in blood red. One was her birth date, and the other the date she would die. It was today's date.

This has to be a joke, thought Darren.

He marked the page with his thumb and flipped through the rest of the book. More photos, more people, and all of them had the dates of their deaths. Some were today, some tomorrow or next week.

Wait! There was his sister, Lenore. Her death would be next month, according to the book. But how? Lenore wasn't sick. She was only six years old. What was going on?

Darren looked back at the photo of Dawn. It had changed. Her skin looked paler, more wrinkled. Her hair wasn't as shiny as it normally was.

He closed the book and shivered. Now it had a title: RECIPES FOR THE BEAST.

A shadow fell across the book. Darren looked up quickly. Something had momentarily blocked out the light from one of the high windows. The shadow again. It was closer this time.

The boy didn't care about putting the book back on the shelf. He leaped over the velvet rope. He raced down row after row. When he reached the door, he stopped to catch his breath.

The people who die in that book, he thought. *Was something going to eat them?*

Darren heard a cry.

He ignored the door. He followed the cries. They grew louder as he neared the center of the hidden library. Turning a corner, he spied a girl lying on the floor. Had she fallen and hurt herself? She was clawing at the carpet. Her feet were stuck inside the lowest shelf of a bookcase. The girl screamed again and moved backward, as if being pulled into the shelf.

The girl's eyes hunted desperately for something to grip. She saw Darren's shoe and looked up. It was Dawn Potter.

"Please," she said.

A growl shook the room. Dawn cried out, and Darren reached down and grabbed her hands.

He pulled, but whatever was pulling from the other side was strong.

"Don't let go!" the girl yelled.

Darren looked at the shelf. A claw at the end of a thick, scaly arm was gripping Dawn's foot. Darren knew it was the beast.

He heard a giggle. The librarian was standing behind him. He pushed his glasses farther up the bridge of his nose and laughed again. "Looks like she'll become part of our permanent collection," he said.

"Help us," said Darren.

"You can't escape that thing," said the librarian. "But don't worry. You can always visit her here in the biographies. She'll make a beautiful addition."

Darren was so angry he released his hold and swung at the guy. He hit him square in the face, sending his glasses flying. The man fell to the floor. He gave Darren an evil look. "You're next," he said.

A scaly hand reached out from the low shelf. The claw gripped the librarian by his hair and began pulling him in. He screamed, louder than Darren thought a person could scream.

"Hurry," said Dawn.

Darren reached down and pulled her to her feet.

The librarian's head had disappeared into the shelf. His legs were kicking wildly. Another growl shook the room, and the man's legs were pulled into the shadows. He was gone.

"Come on," said Darren.

The two ran out of the hidden library. They pulled the wooden door shut behind them and rushed up the stairs to the main floor.

"Are you all right?" Darren asked. They stopped at the top of the steps.

"I don't know," said Dawn. "Maybe."

Patrons wandered around them, gazing into books or glancing at shelves. Students sat at tables with their homework in front of them. Sunlight streamed through the narrow windows. Everything looked normal.

Dawn was catching her breath. "I think . . . ,"

she began, "I think I'm getting an *F* on this assignment."

"Me too," said Darren. "I don't think I could read a book now about someone who was dead."

"Yeah," Dawn agreed. She tried to smile, but Darren felt certain she was going to cry. "I'll — I'll see you at school," she stammered. Then she hurried away.

Darren hadn't told her about the book. The one with her photograph. But things were OK now, right? They had defied the book. Dawn was alive and not dinner for some unknown beast.

The boy felt drained of energy. He needed to get home. He needed to find a place where he wasn't surrounded by books. He walked quickly to the main door of the library. He was reaching for the handle when someone ahead of him opened it for him.

"Thanks," Darren said. It was the librarian!

The man pushed his glasses higher on his nose and smiled. "Librarians don't really go away," he said. "They're always *bound* to come back."

He giggled as Darren ran down the stone steps.

ABOUT THE AUTHOR

Michael Dahl, the author of the Library of Doom and Troll Hunters series, is an expert on fear. He is afraid of heights (but he still flies). He is afraid of small, enclosed spaces (but his house is crammed with over 3,000 books). He is afraid of ghosts (but that same house is haunted). He hopes that by writing about fear, he will eventually be able to overcome his own. So far it is not working. But he is afraid to stop. He claims that, if he had to, he would travel to Mount Doom in order to toss in a dangerous piece of jewelry. Even though he is afraid of volcanoes. And jewelry.

ABOUT THE ILLUSTRATOR

Xavier Bonet is an illustrator and comic-book
artist who resides in Barcelona. Experienced in
2D illustration, he has worked as an animator
and a background artist for several different
production companies. He aims to create works
full of color, texture, and sensation, using
both traditional and digital tools. His work in
children's literature is inspired by magic and
fantasy as well as his passion for the art.

MICHAEL DAHL TELLS ALL

Asking lots of questions might annoy some people, but it is the only way to come up with ideas. Besides, when you're being creative, the only person you're asking questions to is you. Your brain, your imagination. You walk down to the basement and then ask yourself, "What if?" You watch a little boy playing with his dog and you ask, "What would happen?" That's where these stories all began — with a question. A scary question.

THE BOY IN THE BASEMENT

Basements and attics make me nervous. They are the extreme ends of a house, where extreme things might happen. My aunt used to live in a house where the basement was busy with ghostly activity — unexplained footsteps and voices, hands that reached out of nowhere to close doors, unseen things that growled. I told my brain that I needed to come up with a super scary story for the book, and this one popped into my brain. The creepy elements are all there: ghostly children, mysterious messages, noises in the night, and, of course, the basement.

SKIPPY

I recently watched a YouTube video of Japanese robots that look frighteningly human. It's only a matter of time before we start creating robotic animals, before digital dogs and cats will be available at the local pet store. How long will it be before something else small and innocent is built in a factory somewhere?

THE WIZARD OF AHHHHHS!

Our junior high put on a production of *The Wizard of Oz*, and practically the entire seventh grade was cast. Although I was only a general in Emerald City, it was still exciting to be a part of the show. But the rehearsals were long and tiring. Many late nights, my friends and I walked from the dressing room through dark, deserted hallways toward the exit. The backstage of a theater, when all the actors and crew have left, is an eerie, silent place. I used to wonder, if you were alone back there and listened closely, would you hear echoes of shows from long ago? Would you see shadowy figures in costumes glide across the stage?

MEMBER OF THE BAND

My elementary school had several murals in its hallways. I sometimes pretended the painted figures of the students and animals came to life, jumping down to the floor and running into the classrooms. The idea for this story started with the opposite view: What if a living, breathing student became part of the mural? What would it feel like to be flat and part of a wall? Would a mural have its own separate world? How frightening to know that you'd have to stay up there until it was your turn again to be real, until everyone else had their chance.

THE PHANTOM TRAIN

The story of a ghostly train has been pinging around in my brain for a long time. When I was younger, our backyard ended at the railroad tracks. Watching the trains roaring by, day and night, became a part of growing up. One summer, there was a horrible accident at the train crossing a block from our house. A car had smashed into the side of a moving train. The kids of the neighborhood all gathered to survey the wreck. I'll never forget seeing only half a car sitting there on the road. The other half, with the driver, was gone. My imagination produced terrible images of what the driver would look like. I guess those images never left my brain.

THE LIBRARY CLAW

Many creatures feed on old books: paper louses, brown moths, black carpet beetles. What if a similar creature had an unending supply of food in a damp, dark section of a library? How big would it grow? How powerful would it become? The deathwatch beetle can tunnel through a book fifty times its size. I imagined that the bigger one of those tiny gluttons became, the bigger the food they would require. I based the librarian on Batman's foe, the Riddler. He seems like a kooky, spooky, unpredictable character that would giggle, appear suddenly out of thin air, and hide out in a place full of words. Words and stories never die. Perhaps those who live off them are also immortal.

GLOSSARY

banister (BAN-is-tur) — a handrail that runs along the side of stairway

baton (buh-TAHN) — a thin stick that is used by a conductor to direct a band

biography (bye-AH-gruh-fee) — a book that tells the life story of someone other than the author

chrome (KROHM) — a shiny silver metal that is used as a protective covering or for decoration

clarinet (klar-ih-NET) — a long, hollow woodwind instrument that is played by blowing into a mouthpiece that holds a reed and covering holes with the fingers or pressing keys

faithful (FAYTH-fuhl) — loyal

gale (GALE) — a very strong wind

hypnotized (HIP-nuh-tized) — put someone into a state in which the person appears to be asleep but is still able to respond to suggestions and questions

malfunction (mal-FUHNK-shuhn) — a failure to work properly

melody (MEL-uh-dee) — an arrangement of musical notes that makes a tune

mural (MYOOR-uhl) — a large painting on a wall

musician (myoo-ZI-shuhn) — a person who plays, sings, or writes music

refund (ree-FUHND) — a repayment of money

saxophone (SAK-suh-fone) — a wind instrument made of brass, with a mouthpiece that holds a reed, keys for the fingers, and a body that is usually curved

stalking (STAWK-ing) — hunting or tracking a person or an animal in a quiet, secret way

DISCUSSION QUESTIONS

1. In the story "Skippy," we find out that the family pet, Skippy, is actually a robot. Do you think you would like to have a robotic pet? Explain why or why not.

2. Jonica is frightened when she is alone on the stage in the story "The Wizard of AHHHHHs!" Do you think what she saw was real or imagined? Discuss your answer using examples from the text.

3. In the story "The Phantom Train," a man tells Ross and Patricia the story of a haunted stretch of railroad. Would you believe the man if you were Ross or Patricia? Discuss why or why not using examples from the story.

WRITING PROMPTS

1. In "The Library Claw," Darren comes across a photo of his classmate Dawn in a book that lists the date of her death. Darren decides not to tell Dawn what he saw. Imagine an ending to the story where he does tell her, and write that scene.

2. Cameron becomes a part of the mural in the story "Member of the Band." What if, instead of Cam becoming part of the art, someone in the mural had come to life? Write your own version of the story.

3. Natalie finds a spooky note in her closet in "The Boy in the Basement." The note tells her to feed the boy in the basement. Write a letter to Natalie from the perspective of the boy in the basement. What does he want her to know?

MICHAEL DAHL'S
REALLY SCARY STORIES